The Sleuths of Somerville

TOUR OF TROUBLE

Published by Curious Fox, an imprint of Capstone Global Library
Limited, 264 Banbury Road, Oxford, OX2 7DY – Registered company
number: 6695582

www.curious-fox.com

ISBN 978-1-78202-500-9
20 19 18 17 16
10 9 8 7 6 5 4 3 2 1

A CIP catalogue for this book is available from the British Library.

Printed and bound in China.

The Sleuths of Somerville

TOUR OF TROUBLE

by Michele Jakubowski

Curious Fox
a capstone company-publishers for children

CHAPTER ONE

Summer was a busy time at Mick's Diner. Located right off a major road in Somerville, a town so small you'd miss it if you blinked while passing by, it was the perfect place to stop for a good meal in the middle of a long journey.

Fortunately for Amelia and Jason Vega, the owners of Mick's Diner, that's what plenty of people did each summer. Over the years, word had got out about the delicious doughnuts at Mick's, as well as the cheap petrol at Earl's Petrol Station and the appeal of a handful of other places in town. Plenty of travellers marked Somerville on their maps as the place to pause, stretch their legs and take in the town's charm before heading on to bigger, more exciting destinations.

The Vegas' children, 12-year-old Rowan and 11-year-old Astrid, were not as thrilled with summer life in Somerville. They found themselves either frantic while helping out during a rush at the restaurant or bored to tears during the downtimes.

Following the exciting events that had started their summer, the kids now felt that the boring times were here. When two new Somerville residents – 12-year-old Jace and his young mum, Evie – arrived in town, they brought with them plenty of mystery. As Rowan, Astrid and Astrid's best friend, Quinn, befriended Jace, they were curious about the pair and began asking questions and gathering clues. In the end, they learned that Jace and Evie were actually brother and sister, and the two of them had been relocated to Somerville to hide out after their secret agent parents found themselves in trouble. The Vegas, Quinn and her parents, and Somerville Police Captain Joel Osgood rallied around Jace and Evie and vowed to keep their true identities a secret so that they could remain safely in town.

Things settled down quickly after that, and a few weeks later, Evie was enjoying her new job at Mick's Diner and making friends, while Jace had become inseparable from Rowan, Astrid and Quinn. The foursome had fallen into an easy summer routine of helping at the restaurant and hanging out. As the days went on, however, they grew frustrated with the monotony.

Jace and Rowan tried to break up the boredom by starting what they called the Ultimate War Tournament. The boys had been hooked once Mr Vega had taught them the card game, in which the person with the high card wins each round and tries to collect all of his or her opponent's cards. They decided that whoever had the most wins by the end of the summer would be declared the Ultimate War Champion. Astrid and Quinn enjoyed playing sometimes, but Jace and Rowan were way ahead of them. There was plenty of summer left, but they had already begun taunting each other with each victory.

"Winner, winner, chicken dinner!" Jace exclaimed as he scooped up the last of Rowan's cards. Jace beamed as his black hair fell over his pale green eyes.

"Whatever," Rowan grumbled as he added a line under Jace's name on their tally sheet. While Jace and Rowan may have been different in many ways – Jace was tall and laid-back, while Rowan was small for his age and tended to be more serious – neither of them liked to lose.

"Make sure you make that mark nice and dark," Jace continued, teasing his friend. "I'm pretty sure that win puts me in the lead!"

Rowan did some quick counting and frowned when he realized Jace was right. "It's twenty to nineteen," he said. "Let's play again."

Rowan began shuffling the cards, anxious to tie up the score.

Chester Feeney, the longtime mechanic at Earl's Petrol, was sitting near the boys and chuckled at their banter. As Rowan began passing out the cards, Chester went back to reading his *Somerville Gazette*.

Somerville wasn't big enough to have its own daily newspaper, and most people received the *Ledger* from nearby Watertown instead. The *Gazette* was for local news only and came out every two weeks. Despite the fact that most of its news was well-known by the time it came out, most locals enjoyed reading the paper.

"Well, look at that," Chester said, showing the boys the front page. "A bike race is going to come through Somerville."

"Really?" Jace asked excitedly as he put down his cards. "A real race? Which one?"

Jace was a big fan of professional cycling and followed the many races that took place around the world. Having travelled quite a bit with his parents before they were forced into hiding, Jace had attended several major races, including the Giro d' Italia and the Tour de France. He was such a fan he even followed the smaller regional races.

Chester scanned the article again and told Jace, "Says here it's the Tour Across the Land."

"No way!" Jace had abandoned the card game altogether and walked over to Chester to get a better look at the paper. "That's an epic race! It's crazy hard!"

The Tour Across the Land was a long-distance bike race that started in Washington, D.C., and finished four-thousand-eight-hundred kilometres away, in California. It was a gruelling race in which cyclists rode close to one-hundred-and-sixty kilometres each day, often through steep mountain ranges.

Chester went back to the article. "Says here that this stage starts forty-eight kilometres down the main road and will come through Somerville and ride over the mountains before ending up in Watertown. That's no small task! Some of those mountains are treacherous with all the twists and turns in the road. Sounds exciting!"

Chester handed the paper to Jace, who read and re-read the article. "Can you believe it?"

Rowan, who had been re-counting the tallies on their score sheet to make sure the totals were correct, looked up. "Huh? What's that?"

"Were you even listening?" Jace was exasperated. "A super-cool bike race is coming through town in less than two weeks! They'll be riding right in front of the restaurant!"

"Who'll be riding in front of the restaurant?" Astrid asked as she and Quinn walked through the front door. The two words that best described Astrid were "nosy" and "dramatic". These two traits often came together when she felt she was being kept out of the loop about something. Having just returned from delivering boxed lunches, she seemed to be in a particularly nosy mood.

"Tons of famous cyclists!" Jace beamed. "I wonder what teams will be riding?"

Quinn ran her hand through her hair as she glanced at the article. "It's a bike race?" she asked.

"Not just any bike race," Jace replied. He began explaining the skills and training involved in a race of this magnitude, but before he could get very far, Astrid interrupted him.

"So, what you're saying is, you'll spend all this time getting worked up about this race and then we'll sit out front and the riders will whizz by and it will all be over in about ten minutes?"

"No! Well, yes." For a moment Jace was stunned by his friends' lack of interest. "Sort of, but it's so much more than that! In Europe people camp out for days just to get a glimpse of the big races. We get to have one pass by right outside."

His friends stared at him in silence, still waiting to be convinced.

Jace muttered, "Oh, just wait and see! Then you'll understand."

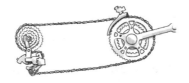

CHAPTER TWO

After Jace gave up on turning his friends into cycling fans and went back to his card game with Rowan, Astrid and Quinn snuck out. They cut through the kitchen on their way upstairs to the apartment the Vegas lived in above the restaurant. The girls were in the midst of hatching a very important plan and wanted to find somewhere private to discuss the details.

Mrs Vega was in the office doing paperwork as the girls walked by.

"Hey!" she called. "How were the deliveries? Is Miss Coco doing okay?"

Mrs Coretta Lownie, or Miss Coco as she was known, was the oldest living resident of Somerville and a regular customer at the restaurant. She was known for spending hours at the counter and chatting endlessly with the lucky, or sometimes unlucky, person who sat beside her. Sometimes her stories were great. Sometimes they were confusing. She could talk for hours.

The restaurant had been noticeably quiet the past few days as Miss Coco stayed home with the sniffles.

"She's doing well," Quinn said. "My dad stopped in and saw her yesterday. He said she's healthier than half the people in town."

Quinn's father was the town doctor and was well aware of the health of the people of Somerville.

"Yep, she's doing great. Gotta go!" Astrid said in a rush as she pulled Quinn towards the back stairs.

"Wait!" Mrs Vega said, wrapping her arms around her daughter. "Did she say when she'd be back? I miss having her around."

Astrid squirmed in her mum's embrace. "She said she'd be back tomorrow. Then she said that you've been skimping on the sugar in the shortbread and she wants you to go back to your old recipe and stop being such a health nut."

Mrs Vega dropped her arms and said with surprise, "She did not say that!"

"Well, no, she didn't," Astrid confessed. "But it is true."

Quinn laughed and said to Mrs Vega, "Miss Coco told us that during the war they had no sugar, so she and her family would have a carrot on a stick for pudding."

"That might actually be true," Mrs Vega said. "During the war there were rations on foods. Families were only allowed so much sugar and other items. They had to come up with some creative substitutes."

Astrid smirked. "She also said that because of eating so many carrots as a child, she now has X-ray vision and can see through the walls of her apartment and watch whatever her neighbours are watching on their TV."

Mrs Vega laughed. "That does sound like something Miss Coco would say. I'm glad she'll be back in tomorrow."

Astrid and Quinn didn't want to be rude, but they were anxious to end the conversation and get away fast. They took small, slow steps backwards towards the stairs.

Mrs Vega noticed their attempt to sneak away. "Where are you two off to in such a hurry?" she asked, suspicious.

The girls exchanged glances before they began talking at the same time.

"We've got this thing," Astrid began.

"Yeah, this important thing," Quinn added.

"But not too important," Astrid said quickly. "I mean, you don't have to worry about it or anything."

"Yep, just this not-too-important thing," Quinn said, following her.

"So, yeah, like, see ya!" Astrid finished, and the pair raced up the stairs.

The Vegas' apartment consisted of the top two floors above Mick's Diner. The first floor of the apartment was a spacious living area that flowed into an open kitchen. Off the back of the kitchen was a utility room and bathroom. The bedrooms were upstairs, along with two more bathrooms and another staircase leading to the rooftop garden.

Having run up two flights of stairs, the girls were panting by the time they entered Astrid's room. Astrid quickly shut the door and turned towards Quinn, who had dropped down on a beanbag chair on the floor.

"So, have you thought of a plan?" she asked.

"I thought you were going to think of a plan and I was going to help you?" Quinn replied.

Astrid flopped onto her bed and sighed. "I couldn't think of anything."

For months, Astrid had been telling her parents that she wanted – no, *needed!* – a mobile phone. A lot of her friends already had one, and if she was going to survive in small-town Somerville, she had to have a way to be connected to the outside world. But so far, nothing had worked.

Astrid's parents were old-fashioned, or "old school", as they referred to themselves, and did not agree that she needed a mobile phone.

"I've tried everything," Astrid moaned. "They won't budge. They said they don't want me walking around like a zombie doing nothing but playing on my phone."

Quinn sat up. "What if you told them you wouldn't be on your phone all the time?"

Astrid looked horrified. "What's the point of having a phone then?"

Quinn shook her head and sunk back down into the chair. "The tricky part for you is that Rowan doesn't even want a phone. He's never going to help you convince them."

"I know. He's too busy playing that silly card game. He doesn't even care about a phone. It's not fair!" Astrid whined.

"Even if they got him one, though, they'd probably make you wait until you're twelve, and then you still wouldn't have a phone right now." Quinn frowned.

"What did your parents say?" Astrid asked. Quinn didn't want a phone in the same way she did, but Astrid thought she would have more leverage with her parents if her best friend had one too. Plus, they could talk all the time that way!

"They said the same thing they always say – not until I'm in high school. I tried your suggestion and asked what I'm supposed to do in case of emergencies, and my dad said, 'You know just about every person in Somerville. If there's an emergency, someone will help you'," Quinn said, doing her best impersonation of her dad.

"It's hopeless!" Astrid exclaimed. "We're going to spend another boring summer here without anything fun to do!"

"Well, we could play another game of War with the boys," Quinn suggested.

Astrid sat up to see if her best friend had gone crazy. When she saw Quinn smiling, she threw a pillow at her and said, "I may be bored, but I'm not *that* bored!"

CHAPTER THREE

"I can't believe I am this bored," Astrid said as she slowly flipped a card from the pile her brother had dealt her.

"Oh, come on! It's fun!" Rowan tried to convince her. He had begged her to play after Jace had beaten him in three straight games the day before. Jace was now up by four games. They had agreed that only games played between Rowan, Jace, Astrid and

Quinn counted towards the tournament. Rowan was so desperate for a few more wins that he told Astrid he would help her to convince their parents to get her a mobile phone if she played with him.

Rowan listened halfheartedly as Astrid went on and on about why she *needed* a mobile phone. She talked endlessly and was barely paying attention to the game, yet every card she flipped was somehow higher than Rowan's. In what felt like the quickest game of War in history, Astrid went through her cards and collected all of Rowan's. He sat stunned, having lost yet another game.

". . . and that's why I really, really need a mobile phone," Astrid said. She was quiet for a moment and then realized they had stopped playing. "Oh, did I win? That was quick."

Rowan felt his face get warm with frustration. But he needed the wins, and to win he needed to play. Between clenched teeth he asked, "Play again?"

"No, thanks," Astrid replied. "Let's talk about how you're going to help me get a phone."

They were sitting in a booth at the back of the restaurant. Mr Vega was across the restaurant, replenishing the bakery case. Rowan leaned out of the booth and yelled, "Dad! I think you should get Astrid a phone, okay?"

Without even looking up from what he was doing, Mr Vega replied, "No can do, son. Nice try, though!"

Now Astrid was the furious one. "That's it? I thought you were going to help me!"

Rowan shrugged. "I totally tried. Ready for another game?"

Astrid stood up and stormed off.

Rowan debated not writing down Astrid's win on the tally sheet, but in the end, he did. He decided that it would make his victory that much sweeter when he won the Ultimate War Tournament.

He was so busy tallying the results that he didn't notice when two men came into the restaurant and sat at the booth behind him. He didn't mean to eavesdrop, but that's just what he did when he heard what they were talking about.

"I don't know how you did it, Victor, but this place is perfect!" said one of the men.

"I know," the man who must have been Victor said smugly. "It wasn't easy convincing the race organizers, but bringing the riders through this teeny town is just perfect. Plus, finishing the stage in Watertown will get us lots of exposure."

Rowan realized that these guys must be connected to the Tour Across the Land. Jace wasn't expected in for a while, so Rowan decided to see what he could find out for his friend. Maybe he could get him some behind-the-scenes access to the race.

As he stood up from his booth, he saw Evie walking towards the men with some menus. He took the menus from her and said, "I've got this one."

She looked confused, but didn't argue.

"Welcome to Mick's Diner," Rowan said cheerfully to the men. "Have you ever eaten here before?"

Rowan gave the men a once-over. Both were big men, slightly older than his parents. Neither man had a full head of hair or a smile on his face. Both wore brown jackets with green lettering on the front that read "Big Root Tree Company".

They each snatched a menu from Rowan's hands and began scanning the pages. Without looking up, the man on the right mumbled, "We're not from around here."

No kidding, thought Rowan.

"Our special today is steak and ale pie," Rowan told them. "It comes with mashed potatoes, gravy and a side of steamed vegetables."

The man on the left, who was slightly bigger and had a bushy moustache, tossed his menu back at Rowan and snapped, "We'll take two of those and two coffees."

The man on the right slumped his shoulders, disappointed that he didn't get to order his own meal. He sighed as he handed his menu back to Rowan.

Moustache Man must be in charge, Rowan thought to himself.

"So, are you in town for the bike race?" Rowan asked casually.

In unison, both men turned their heads slowly to look at Rowan for the first time since he'd approached the table. Their eyes were wide with surprise. It was then that Rowan realized he only knew this information because he had been eavesdropping. He quickly added, "We've been getting a lot of people in here lately because of the race."

The men relaxed a bit but didn't get any friendlier. Moustache Man couldn't hide his impatience as he told Rowan, "Our company is sponsoring this stage of the race. We came through to check out the route."

Rowan beamed. These men may not be the nicest guys on Earth, but if they were involved with the race, maybe they could help Jace and Rowan meet some of the riders. Maybe they could even get some autographs and pictures with them.

"That's so cool," Rowan began. "My friend Jace is a huge cycling fan! He would love to –"

"That's great, kid," Moustache Man said, cutting him off. "How about you put our order in now. We're getting hungry."

"Um, sure," Rowan responded. He hung his head as he walked away. He decided not to push it with the men. Maybe they'd come back and be in a better mood, and he could try talking to them again.

Rowan put the order in and told Evie she could have her table back. With a frown he told her, "But don't expect a good tip."

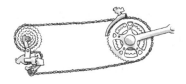

CHAPTER FOUR

Quinn and Astrid were delivering lunches and making their last stop at the Sugar Shack, the local patisserie and sweet shop. They saved this stop for last because they loved hanging out with Delilah Doherty, the shop's owner. Delilah had been born and raised in Somerville, but had studied baking and sweet-making in Paris before opening her shop. Quinn and Astrid thought Delilah was very cool and interesting. They especially liked how she treated them like peers rather than like little kids.

"And they won't even talk about it anymore! They said, 'End of discussion.' It's so not fair!" Astrid was, yet again, telling her sad story of how her parents wouldn't get her a mobile phone.

"Parents can be like that," Delilah said. "Trust me, you'll never be too old for them to tell you what to do."

"Really?" Quinn asked. "But you're an adult. What do your parents tell you what to do?"

"Plenty!" Delilah responded. At 26, Delilah was the only one of the six Doherty girls not yet married, a fact her parents never let her forget. Delilah knew all about parents and their unwelcome advice. She glanced quickly at the clock on the wall and added, "Well, I've taken up enough of your time. You girls better get back to work."

"We're in no rush," Astrid said. "We always save your delivery for last."

"Then we're done for the day," Quinn added.

A quick look of panic crossed Delilah's face. She glanced at the clock again. "Well, as much as I'd love to spend the afternoon with you two, I've got a bunch of boring paperwork to do. How much do I owe you for lunch?"

Astrid reached into the insulated bag they used to transport the lunches. "That's weird. There are two lunches in here. I was sure this was our last stop. Who could the other lunch be for?"

Delilah blushed slightly and said, "They're both for me." When Quinn and Astrid gave her puzzled looks, she shrugged and added, "I was feeling extra hungry when I ordered!"

Delilah opened the till and quickly took out some money. As she handed the notes to the girls she guided them towards the door. "Thanks again, girls. Keep the change. Great chatting with you!"

Quinn and Astrid stood on the pavement in front of the Sugar Shack, feeling a little stunned by their abrupt departure.

"What should we do now?" Quinn asked.

"I guess we should head back to the restaurant. I need to drop off the delivery bag," Astrid replied.

As they headed back towards the restaurant, Police Captain Joel Osgood came hurrying around the corner, almost walking right into them.

"Hey, Captain," Astrid said. "Is everything okay?"

Joel Osgood was an army veteran and the youngest police captain in the town's history. While some of the older police officers weren't happy about being passed over by a much younger man, they all had to agree that he was great at his job and an asset to the community.

"Oh! Sorry about that!" Captain Osgood looked flustered. "Everything's fine. I'm just late, for, uh, an appointment."

"We won't keep you," Quinn said. "Have fun at your, uh, appointment."

Captain Osgood smiled and nodded and hurried down the street.

"That was strange," Astrid said as the pair continued heading back towards the restaurant.

With nothing planned for the rest of the day, neither of them was in a hurry. They walked at a slow pace, kicking rocks back and forth and looking into the shop windows.

They were right in front of the restaurant when Astrid brought her foot back to kick an object on the pavement. Before she kicked, however, she looked down and realized what it was.

"Oh my gosh!" she exclaimed and picked up the object. "It's a phone!"

Astrid looked closer and noticed that it was an older-model smartphone. She didn't care how old it might be – it was a phone and it was in her hand!

Quinn looked at the mobile phone in her friend's hand. "Don't be too excited. It might be a phone, but it belongs to someone else."

Astrid knew this but chose to be excited anyway. "But this has got to be, like, a sign or something. Don't you think?"

Quinn didn't think that at all, but kept her mouth shut.

"Let's drop off the bag and go up to my room and figure out who it belongs to," Astrid said, determined to turn this find into a way to get a phone of her own. "Maybe the owner will want to reward me by giving it to me."

Despite her doubts, Quinn still didn't say anything and followed Astrid into the restaurant.

As they walked in, Jace and Rowan called them over to where they were sitting at the counter.

"We need your help," Rowan told them.

"Oh, sure," Astrid replied sourly. "Just like you helped me with Mum and Dad?"

Rowan frowned at his sister. "This is for Jace. And you're not getting a phone, so just get over it."

Jace spoke up before Rowan ruined any chance they had of getting Quinn and Astrid to help them. "A couple of guys were in here recently, and Rowan heard them talking about the bike race. He said they were wearing Big Root Tree Company jackets, so I looked into it, and they are sponsoring this stage of the race."

"Okay," Quinn said. "So what exactly do you need from us?"

"We haven't seen them since, but we're hoping they come in again," Jace began. "Since they are connected to the race, we're hoping we can meet some of the riders."

Jace loved to talk about cycling, and he launched into an explanation of how the riders were divided up into teams. The team he liked most was Indulge Cycling, which featured his favourite rider, Jan Eldridge. Among his least favourite riders was Jacque Bolive, a Frenchman who had once been a top rider before finding himself in trouble with the cycling community. Jace explained how the Tour Across the Land would be the first race back for Jacque after his fall from grace.

"If you see them here or anywhere else, will you let us know?" Jace asked.

Astrid could feel the phone in her back pocket and was anxious to get upstairs and find out who its owner was. "Yeah, sure, whatever. We'll keep an eye out, no problem," she said dismissively.

"We're serious, Astrid," Rowan snapped, unhappy with his sister's attitude.

"Um, guys?" Quinn said.

"And I was serious when I asked for your help!" Astrid replied loudly.

The pair immediately launched into a back-and-forth shouting match.

"Hey! Hey!" Jace stood up and got between the quarrelsome siblings. "Stop it, you two!"

But Astrid and Rowan's arguing grew more and more heated.

"Guys?" Quinn said a little louder.

Astrid and Rowan kept fighting, while Jace did his best to get them to stop. Quinn grew tired of being ignored, and in a much louder, more authoritative voice she shouted, "Guys!"

Astrid, Rowan and Jace fell silent, all three of them shocked by Quinn's tone and her volume.

"Don't look," she said. "But the guys you were talking about are here."

Before the words were out of Quinn's mouth, her friends all turned and looked in that direction. Quinn rolled her eyes at their inability to follow directions. She leaned in and whispered, "They're in the back booth, near the toilets."

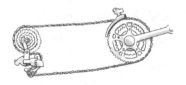

CHAPTER FIVE

The group agreed that it would probably be best if only Jace and Rowan went over to the table where the men from the Big Root Tree Company were sitting.

Astrid was off in a flash, but before leaving, Quinn said, "Good luck! Let us know if we can do anything to help."

Jace thanked her and stood up.

"Hold on a second," Rowan said, grabbing Jace's arm. "We can't just run over there. Those guys were very grumpy when I saw them. Let them eat their lunch, and then we can bring them over some pudding to soften them up. My mum made lemon bars this morning."

"Good idea," Jace said. He waited and watched as the men ate their meals. To anyone else it would look like the men were quickly shovelling down their food, but to Jace it felt like they were taking forever.

When the man with the moustache finally pushed away his empty plate, Rowan nodded to Jace. In a flash, Rowan grabbed a fresh pot of coffee, while Jace put lemon bars on two plates. As they made their way over to the table they could hear the men talking as they spread out a large map on the table.

"This map is useless," grunted one of the men. "We drove up and down that mountain and still couldn't find that place."

Rowan cleared his throat to get their attention. "How was your meal? Would you like some pudding?"

Jace put down the plates as Rowan refilled their coffee cups. Before they could say another word, the man without the moustache snapped, "Get lost, kid. We're busy!"

The boys were shocked. They turned to walk away, but the other man held up his hand to stop them. "Hang on a second, guys." He gave them a very unnatural-looking smile and asked, "You boys are from around here, right?"

"Yes," Rowan told him.

"He's lived here his whole life, and I live here now, too," Jace said in a rush.

The non-moustached man looked confused but didn't say a word.

"You said something about being cycling fans, right?" Moustache Man said as he popped a toothpick into his mouth.

"Yes!" Jace practically shouted.

Moustache Man twirled his toothpick and nodded. "Good, good. I'm Victor, and this is my partner, Lenny. We own the Big Root Tree Company. Our company is sponsoring this stage of the race, the one that passes right outside here."

Jace couldn't contain himself. "I know every rider in the race, like Jan Eldridge and Lorenzo Ferrari. I heard even Jacque Bolive will be riding!"

Jace rattled on and on about the difficulty of the course this year and the different challenges the riders would face.

Rowan nudged Jace, who finally stopped talking. He was used to Astrid rambling, but this was the first time he'd heard Jace do it.

"Yeah, that's great, kid. What are your names?" Moustache Man asked.

Rowan introduced them both and explained that his parents owned the restaurant.

Victor ate his lemon bar in two giant bites and put the toothpick back in his mouth. "So you guys are pretty familiar with the town, I suppose? We need some help navigating part of the route."

"We can definitely help!" Rowan told him. He looked over at Jace, who nodded.

"Great," Victor smiled, obviously pleased with himself. "We'll meet you back here tomorrow at lunchtime."

"Sounds good," Jace said.

"See ya," Rowan added.

Rowan and Jace tried to act cool as they walked away, but as soon as they walked into the kitchen they let out a cheer that could be heard throughout the restaurant.

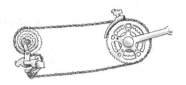

CHAPTER SIX

Always one for dramatic flair, Astrid sat on the floor, facing Quinn with the phone between them. After several minutes of sitting and watching the blank screen, Quinn got frustrated.

"Aren't you even going to pick it up?" she asked. "We've got to find out who it belongs to."

Astrid took a deep breath and picked up the phone as if it were a precious object. "I can't believe I finally have a phone," she said, stroking the phone. "It's as if fate wanted me to have one."

"What are you talking about?" Quinn rolled her eyes. "First of all, you still don't have a phone, because this one belongs to someone else. And second, what's all this 'fate' talk?"

"Don't you think this is a sign that I should have a phone?" Astrid asked.

"No." Quinn was tired of keeping her mouth shut. "I think a lot of people eat at your parents' restaurant each day and one of them dropped their phone."

Astrid let out a yelp as Quinn snatched the phone out of her hand.

Quinn didn't have a phone of her own, but she'd spent enough time playing with her parents' to know how to use one. Astrid leaned over and watched wide-eyed, trying to get a glimpse of what Quinn was doing.

"Hmmm," Quinn finally said. "The number of the phone isn't a local one, so it probably doesn't belong to anyone from Somerville."

"Good!" Astrid sat back and clapped her hands. "Maybe it belongs to a rich, kind tourist who has lots of phones already and will just tell me to keep this one out of the goodness of his heart."

Quinn stopped what she was doing and looked up, giving Astrid a look that could only be interpreted to mean: *Are you joking?*

Astrid ignored the look and remained optimistic. "What else did you find?"

Quinn tapped a few more times on the phone's screen. "That's weird," she said. "There is only one contact stored."

"One contact?" Astrid said. "They must not use their phone very much. They probably won't even miss it!"

Quinn rolled her eyes and put the phone up to her ear.

Frantically, Astrid sat forward. "What are you doing?" she asked.

"I'm calling the contact," Quinn replied. "It's the only way to find out who owns this phone."

Astrid stood up and paced. She wasn't ready to leave her fantasy world where the owner was a rich traveller with no friends who would happily give Astrid one of his phones. "Put it on speaker," she ordered.

Quinn tapped the screen and a ringing sound filled the room.

"What?" a girl's voice snapped, causing them both to jump.

"Um, hello?" Quinn said with trepidation.

There was a long pause and then, "Who is this?"

"Our names are Quinn and Astrid and we found this phone," Quinn explained.

There was another long pause before the girl said, "So why are you calling me?"

"Well, you were the only contact saved in it," Quinn explained.

The girl let out a loud laugh. "The only contact? Figures. How lame!"

Quinn shrugged her shoulders and mouthed to Astrid, *"What now?"*

Astrid stopped pacing and sat down across from Quinn. "Do you know who this phone belongs to?"

"Who did you say you were?" The girl sounded unsure.

"Our names are Astrid and Quinn, and we live in Somerville," Astrid explained. "I found this phone in front of my parents' restaurant."

"Oh!" the girl exclaimed. "Is that the place with the amazing doughnuts? We always stop there!"

"That's the place," Astrid said. She then added, "So, about the phone . . ."

The girl laughed again. "It belongs to my little brother, Gus. He must have dropped it when we were going back to the car. He's a total lummox."

"What's your name?" Quinn asked.

"Maddie," the girl replied.

Quinn and Astrid went on to discover that Maddie was also eleven years old and that her family stopped in Somerville often when they travelled.

After chatting a bit, Quinn asked, "Do you want us to post the phone back to Gus?"

Before she could stop herself, Astrid reached over and punched Quinn in the arm.

"Ouch!" Quinn cried.

"Is everything okay?" Maddie asked.

Quinn glared at Astrid, who glared right back.

"She's fine," Astrid responded. "You said Gus is such a lummox. He'll probably never miss his phone, right?"

Now it was Quinn's turn to reach over and punch Astrid in the arm.

"He'll notice eventually," Maddie told them. "He'd be in so much trouble if my parents knew he lost it. I can't wait to tell him. He'll owe me big time for keeping my mouth shut!"

Quinn and Astrid laughed as they rubbed their sore arms.

"Don't post it yet, though," Maddie said. "We're on holiday, and our post is on hold."

"Holiday?" Astrid asked. "You are so lucky!"

Maddie replied doubtfully, "You think so?"

"Yes!" Astrid and Quinn said in unison.

"We're stuck here with nothing to do all summer," Quinn told her. "You're so lucky you get to travel!"

"Where are you going for your holiday?" Astrid asked. "I bet it's somewhere exciting and glamorous!"

"Um, we're going to . . ." Maddie paused before continuing. "Paris."

"Paris?" Quinn practically shouted.

"You are *so* lucky!" Astrid confirmed.

"Yeah, well, then we're headed to London and a few other places. It's no big deal," Maddie said casually.

Quinn and Astrid both sighed with envy. Their summer plans didn't involve leaving Somerville.

"I'll tell you what," Maddie said. "Hang on to the phone while we're gone. I'll call you from our trip and tell you all about what we're doing. It will be like you're with me!"

"Really?" Astrid cried. She might not be getting a phone, but it certainly would be cool to hear firsthand about an amazing worldwide trip like the one Maddie was going on.

"No problem," Maddie said. "I'll call and text you when I can. It will be so much fun!"

The girls chatted a few more minutes before Maddie had to go. After hanging up, Quinn and Astrid looked at each other and squealed, "We're going to Paris!"

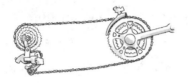

CHAPTER SEVEN

The next day Jace and Rowan were anxious as they waited for Victor and Lenny to finish their lunches. After Rowan had refilled their coffee three times and they'd each eaten two helpings of lemon meringue pie, the men were ready to talk about the race.

Victor let out a loud burp and said, "Here's what we need from you two: Do you know how to get to Raven's Point?"

Jace had never heard of Raven's Point, so he turned to look at Rowan. He did not like the look on his friend's face.

"Why do you want to know how to get to Raven's Point?" Rowan asked. "I went over the race route last night, and Raven's Point is almost a kilometre from where the riders are going to be on Becker Mountain. In fact, Raven's Point is a mountain pass that is so dangerous, even hikers aren't allowed on it. Maybe you're thinking of somewhere else?"

Victor's face reddened. He puffed his cheeks and exhaled loudly before giving the boys one of his creepy smiles. "Do you know how to get there or not?"

"Well, yes," Rowan replied. "But it's very dangerous. There are signs all over the place warning people to stay away."

Victor sat up straight and said, "Exactly!"

Lenny jumped in his seat, wrinkling his eyebrows in confusion about his partner's sudden enthusiasm. But he didn't say anything.

Victor went on. "We want the riders to be safe, so we're checking out any hazards to make sure they steer clear of them."

Lenny smiled and nodded his head in agreement as he muttered, "Yeah, that's it."

"I really don't think anyone would confuse Raven's Point for part of the course," Rowan replied. "Even if they somehow stumbled upon it, I doubt they'd want to climb it!"

"Look, kid, we just want to make sure for ourselves," Victor glared at Rowan.

"Uh, okay," Rowan said, looking tentatively at Jace. He knew how much his friend wanted to be a part of this race, so he said, "We can show you. Our bikes are out front. Meet us at Perkin's Outlook. Just take the High Street to West Road towards the mountain and follow the signs."

The men agreed to the plan and headed to the counter to pay their bill.

Rowan and Jace rode off towards Becker Mountain, part of the range that stood between Somerville and nearby Watertown. Somerville was situated on the slope of Becker Mountain, while Watertown was located in the valley below. Perkin's Outlook was a paved area off the main road that offered a gorgeous view of Watertown and beyond. A half-kilometre from Perkin's Outlook was Raven's Point, the highest part of Becker Mountain. While the view might have been even better at Raven's Point, getting there was an extremely dangerous climb, and one misstep could lead to a fall off a sheer drop of more than thirty metres.

Rowan knew several trails that made the ride up to Perkin's Outlook quicker by bike than by car. When the pair reached the outlook, they stood looking at the stunning view and catching their breath.

"Wow," Jace said, taking a drink of water.

"Yeah," Rowan agreed. "The view is pretty spectacular."

They stood quietly for another moment before Rowan turned towards Jace. "I still don't understand why they want to find Raven's Point."

Jace shrugged. "To keep their riders safe, I guess. A stranger might not know where to put hazard signs and stuff like that."

"Seems strange, though," Rowan said. "I don't see why the riders would have any reason to go off the route and up to a dangerous cliff in the first place."

Before Jace could respond, a brown pickup truck with green lettering on the side that read "Big Root Tree Company" pulled up and parked in the small lot next to the outlook.

Victor popped a fresh toothpick into his mouth as he and Lenny approached the boys.

"So, where's this Raven's Point place?" Victor said without even glancing towards the scenic view below.

"This way," Rowan directed as they headed farther up the mountain.

The two men were sorely out of shape, and Rowan and Jace quickly pulled ahead of them. When Rowan noticed how far ahead they had got, they stopped to let the men catch up. As Victor and Lenny got closer, the boys could hear pieces of their conversation.

"This is pretty hard to climb," Lenny panted. "Are you sure Jacque will do it?"

"He'll do it," Victor grunted. "That's why we're paying him. If it was easy, we'd do it ourselves."

"What about the beetles?" Lenny asked.

The wind shifted direction so Rowan and Jace couldn't hear Victor's response, but they could see his face as he got closer. He appeared to be barking at Lenny, who sheepishly hung his head and kept climbing.

"'Beetles'? Is that a cycling term?" Rowan whispered sarcastically to Jace.

"If it is, I've never heard it. Maybe we didn't hear that right," Jace responded. "I wonder if the Jacque they are talking about is Jacque Bolive?"

Rowan and Jace climbed to a place where they could see the top of Raven's Point in the near distance. There were signs posted all around that read, "Danger!", "Keep Out" and "Do Not Pass!" Just beyond the signs, the trail ended and the climb to the top became steeper and more uneven, eventually turning into a wall of sharp rocks. Even an experienced mountain climber would have thought twice before trying to reach the top of Raven's Point.

They waited just below the final ascent to Raven's Point as the two men slowly made their way up. When they reached Jace and Rowan, the men were winded and their faces were beetroot red.

"There's Raven's Point up there," Rowan informed them as he pointed up the hectic-looking climb. "It's so dangerous no one is allowed to go to the top. I'm pretty sure your riders are smart enough to stay away. Even if they could make that climb, one wrong step at the top and they'd fall to their death."

"You can never be too careful," Victor grunted and took a step towards the cliff. He made it a step past Rowan and stumbled as the rocks shifted beneath his feet.

Rowan grabbed Victor's arm to steady him and warned, "I wouldn't go any farther if I was you."

Victor shook off the help and snapped at Lenny, "Get up there and make sure it's the right place."

As much as he wanted to be a part of the bike race and meet the riders, Jace realized that these two men were up to no good. Were they trying to find a shortcut for Jacque? If so, they had picked a potentially deadly one. "The right place for what?" he asked. "What's going on here?"

Victor glared at him, and Jace worried that he might have crossed the line. Lenny stood nearby, pacing nervously as he looked up at the side of the mountain. No one spoke for a moment as Victor looked like he was deciding what to do next.

Finally he flashed his fake smile and said, "Nothing's going on here. Let's head back."

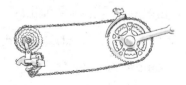

CHAPTER EIGHT

Jace and Rowan said a hasty goodbye to Victor and Lenny at the outlook and raced back to the restaurant. When they got there they found Astrid and Quinn sitting in a booth looking at a small object between them on the table. As the boys got closer, Astrid snatched up whatever it was they were looking at and put it in her pocket. The boys were too amped up about their trip to Raven's Point to ask questions.

"You are not going to believe what just happened!" Rowan said as they slid into the booth. He and Jace proceeded to take turns telling the girls about their adventurous outing to Raven's Point.

"You went to Raven's Point?" Astrid asked. "Mum and Dad are going to kill you!"

Rowan shot Astrid a dirty look and said, "We didn't try to climb it. I'm not stupid!"

Quinn spoke up quickly before the pair could start fighting. "What do you think is going on?" Aside from finding the phone, this was the most exciting thing that had happened all week.

"I don't know, but something is definitely up," Jace replied.

"We're going to research the Big Root Tree Company and see if we can find anything out," Rowan said.

"Sounds fun!" Quinn smiled. "We'll help!"

Just then a muffled buzzing could be heard. Astrid jumped up and pushed Rowan out of her way so she could get out of the booth.

"Let's go, Quinn!" she said.

Rowan gave his sister a suspicious look. "What is going on with you?"

"Nothing!" she replied quickly. "We'll help you with the investigation in a little while. Right now we've got something else to do."

Astrid couldn't keep still and practically pulled Quinn out of the booth. Before they left, Quinn asked, "Where should we meet you?"

"We're going to my house. My internet connection is better," Jace said.

"See you there!" Astrid called, racing off.

Quinn and Astrid sprinted up the three flights of stairs to get to the rooftop balcony above the Vegas' apartment. Astrid pulled the phone out of her back pocket as she flopped onto a deckchair.

"Hello?" she said breathlessly as she answered the phone.

"Put it on speaker!" Quinn whispered.

Astrid touched the speaker button on the phone. Maddie's voice said, "Bonjour, girls!"

Astrid and Quinn squealed with delight!

"You're in Paris already?" Quinn asked. "That was so fast!"

"Um, yeah," Maddie started. "We, uh, we took a private jet so we travelled really fast."

Maddie told Astrid and Quinn all the details about her trip to Paris, including their fancy hotel located next to the Eiffel Tower and the scrumptious croissants she enjoyed each morning for breakfast.

Astrid's eyes widened. "Wow! That is so cool!"

"Can you send us pictures?" Quinn asked.

The phone went silent, and they were worried they'd lost their connection. Finally, they heard Maddie say, "Sure! I'll send them after we hang up."

"How long are you staying in Paris?" Astrid asked.

"Oh, not long. Then we're off to London," Maddie replied. "What's up with you guys?"

"Not much," Astrid confessed. "There is this silly bike race coming through town soon, and these weird guys have been coming into the restaurant. They've been asking all sorts of weird questions."

Quinn and Astrid went on to tell Maddie what they knew about the race and Victor and Lenny. They all agreed that something strange was definitely going on, and Maddie made the girls promise to fill her in on any details they uncovered.

"I'd better get going," Maddie said. "I'll talk to you guys soon!"

"Don't forget the pictures!" Astrid said just before hanging up.

"That was so cool," Quinn said. "Maddie is the luckiest kid ever!"

"I know," Astrid agreed.

Suddenly, the phone buzzed again. A message on the screen let them know that they had received two pictures. Astrid tapped on the phone to reveal images of the Eiffel Tower and a flaky croissant on a plate.

"So cool," Quinn said again as they headed out to meet the boys.

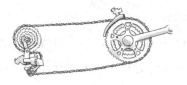

CHAPTER NINE

The Potters' place was an enormous old house located on a hill outside of Somerville. It was a legend in town due to the many stories about its original owners, the Potter family, and their mysterious disappearance from Somerville decades ago.

The current residents were Evie and Jace, and the old Potter house had been refurbished into a comfortable, modern dwelling by the National Intelligence Agency. The agency needed a place for Evie and Jace to hide out while their parents were still in danger.

While Quinn, Astrid and Rowan had once been afraid to step foot in the mysterious old house, they now loved spending time there. The NIA had made sure Jace and Evie had all they needed and more.

When Astrid and Quinn arrived, they found Jace and Rowan sitting in front of two large flat-screen computer monitors.

"Find anything interesting yet?" Quinn asked as she and Astrid stood behind the boys to get a view of the screens.

"Nope," Jace said as he scrolled down on the page they were looking at, which Astrid and Quinn saw was the Big Root Tree Company website.

"The website says the company is from Watertown. Looks like they specialize in planting new trees. In fact, they've got some awful reviews. Customers complained that they wouldn't treat their diseased trees and always insisted on pulling them out and planting new ones," Rowan informed them.

"What does that have to do with the bike race?" Astrid asked.

"Not much," Jace said, frowning. "Let's see what we can find out about Jacque Bolive. Maybe he has something to do with this."

With a few clicks on the keyboard, Jace quickly pulled up a list of search results for Jacque Bolive. As they skimmed through them, Jace read aloud bits and pieces about Jacque's rise to fame as a young superstar in the cycling world, and how that success was snatched away due to his poor sportsmanship and questionable training practices. He had been banned from cycling for five years and was now trying to make a comeback. So far his return to cycling had not been popular with fans.

"It's kind of strange that he would ride for a team as small as CBC Cycling. But then again, none of the big teams would have him after all his troubles," Jace said.

"Sounds like a great guy," Rowan said sarcastically.

Jace shrugged his shoulders. "The sad thing is, if he hadn't been such an idiot, he could have been a huge star."

Astrid leaned over Rowan's shoulder to get a better look at the screen. A thin, muscular young man with a buzzed haircut and smirk on his face stared back at her. "He even looks like a cheater," she remarked.

Just then a buzzing came from her pocket. She went to grab the phone to silence it, but Rowan was quicker and grabbed it from her hand.

"Hey!" Astrid shouted as Rowan jumped up and moved out of her reach.

"Where did you get this?" he asked as he ran to the other side of the room.

Astrid chased after him and shouted, "Give it back! It's mine!"

Rowan was not about to give the phone back to his sister, and as she got closer to him he tapped on the screen, ending the buzzing. "Hello?" he said.

Astrid stopped in her tracks as a look of panic

came across her face. The room was silent for a moment before Maddie's voice came from the phone. "Hello? Who is this?"

Rowan had answered using the speakerphone, so Quinn and Astrid both rushed closer to him and shouted, "It's us, Maddie!"

"Okay," Maddie spoke slowly. "What's going on here?"

Rowan looked at the phone in his hand as if he were holding a ticking time bomb. "That's what I want to know," he said.

"Who is that?" Maddie asked. "Astrid? Quinn? Are you there?"

"They're here," Rowan said and darted out of the way as Astrid lurched for the phone. He may not have known what was going on, but he certainly enjoyed watching his sister freak out about it.

"This is Rowan," he said as he zigzagged out of Astrid's reach. When she and Quinn had him cornered, he tossed the phone to Jace on the other side of the room.

"And this is Jace," Jace laughed, enjoying their game of keep-away. As Astrid ran towards him he noticed that she looked as though she was about to cry. Unlike Rowan, who would have considered that a victory, Jace felt bad and handed her the phone.

"Aw, man!" Rowan shouted and began laughing.

"Hi, Maddie!" Astrid said, out of breath. "I'm so sorry about that!"

"No problem," Maddie giggled. "Are those the boys you told me about?"

"Yes," Astrid replied as she glared at Rowan. "One is nice and the other is my brother."

"How does she know who we are?" Rowan asked. "What is going on here? Where did you get a phone?"

"Maddie's brother dropped his phone in front of the restaurant, and Astrid found it," Quinn explained. "They're on holiday now, and we're going to send it back when they get home. Until then, she's been calling to tell us about her trip."

"They're in Paris now!" Astrid said proudly, as if she were on the trip, too.

"Paris is cool," Jace said. "Have you been to the Catacombs yet?"

"Um, yeah," Maddie responded uncertainly. "I think we ate dinner there last night."

Jace tried to hold back a laugh as he explained, "I doubt it. The Catacombs are a bunch of tunnels filled with the skulls and skeletons of about six million people. Some people call it the world's largest grave. It sounds creepy, but it's actually pretty cool."

Maddie laughed a nervous chuckle and muttered, "I must be thinking of something else."

"You should check it out," Jace said.

Maddie quickly changed the subject. "Did you find anything out about those tree guys?"

Rowan gave Astrid a look that let her know that he wasn't pleased Maddie knew about their investigation. She ignored the look and told Maddie, "Not much. They seem kind of shady, but we still don't know what they are up to."

"Well, good luck," Maddie said. "I'd better get going. Nice meeting you, Rowan and Jace."

They all said goodbye, and as soon as Astrid hung up the phone, Rowan pounced. "Do Mum and Dad know about this phone?"

"Well, not exactly," Astrid admitted. She really didn't want Rowan ruining this for her. Then she remembered something. "Just like they don't know about you going to Raven's Point."

Rowan flinched, knowing how furious his parents would be if they knew he'd gone up there. "I'll make you a deal. I won't tell Mum and Dad about the phone if you won't tell them about me going to Raven's Point twice."

"Twice?" Astrid asked.

"Yep. Before we left, Victor and Lenny asked us to take Jacque up there. Jace wants to meet Jacque, and I'm hoping we can get some information out of him about what's going on," Rowan explained.

Astrid wasn't keen on her brother and Jace going up to Raven's Point again, but she didn't want to lose the phone she considered hers, either.

"Deal?" Rowan asked, extending his hand.

Astrid shook her brother's hand. "Deal."

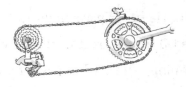

CHAPTER TEN

Jace believed Jacque Bolive could have been a legend in the cycling world if it weren't for his arrogance and laziness. Professional cycling is a team sport, and although only one rider crosses the finish line first, it takes the work of the entire team to make it happen.

For five years, Jacque rode for Indulge Cycling, and for the final three years with them, he was the rider whom the others helped to finish first. He had worked hard and kept quiet for the first two years, but once he earned that top spot, he became a nightmare to ride with. He never gave credit to his teammates and demanded special treatment. He began to skimp on his training, and as his performance suffered, he grew desperate and resorted to cheating during races. His teammates were tired of his attitude and were glad when racing officials caught him and banned him from professional cycling for five years.

Despite his shady past, Jace was still excited to meet such an accomplished rider. Jace was nervous as he and Rowan waited for Jacque to arrive at Perkin's Outlook. Forty-five minutes after their scheduled meeting time, a cheap, compact rental car rattled up the mountain and turned into the car park.

"I expected a professional athlete to drive a nicer car," Rowan whispered.

"Rumour is he's flat broke," Jace responded. Although Jacque made a lot of money riding and had earned several endorsement deals, he'd frittered away his fortune on his extravagant, and often wasteful, lifestyle. After he was banned, all of his endorsement deals dried up, and he was left with nothing. Some people said he didn't even want to ride again but was in need of the money and uninterested in finding a new career.

Without even looking in the boys' direction, Jacque climbed out of his car and snapped, "So, where is this place?"

Jacque was tall and slim, and his legs were pure muscle. He was in great shape, partly because he wanted to ride well and partly because he wanted to look good.

"Hello, Mr Bolive. It's an honour to meet you," Jace said, extending his hand.

Jacque gave Jace a strange look before shaking his hand. "Sure, kid. Can we hurry this up? Today's my first rest day in a week, and I've already wasted half of it driving here."

"Um, sure, right this way," Jace said as he tried not to be rattled by Jacque's rudeness. He knew that riders in professional races, especially ones as demanding as this, were given a rest day only about once a week. Most riders spent the day off their feet and having their legs massaged. Jace was aware of the fact that Jacque's team was several minutes behind his former team, Indulge Cycling, and was surprised that Jacque wasn't at the hotel resting.

Jacque was in much better shape than Victor and Lenny. For a stretch he jogged ahead of the boys. Rowan and Jace struggled to catch up with him.

"It's pretty cool that you're riding in the Tour Across the Land," Jace said, trying to strike up a conversation.

Jacque rolled his eyes and mumbled, "If you think so."

Jace tried again. "I saw you ride in the Tour of the Gila. I was only five, but I totally remember watching you finish a stage. You were amazing."

Jacque didn't bother responding and instead picked up the pace again to get ahead of Rowan and Jace.

"Be careful!" Rowan warned as they neared Raven's Point. Much like Victor had, Jacque ignored the warning signs and walked right past them. Also like Victor, he slipped and nearly stumbled. Jacque spewed a string of French curse words. Jace and Rowan needed all their strength to keep from laughing.

Jacque regained his composure. "So, it's right up there? Just climb these rocks?"

Rowan nodded his head.

"And what's at the top?" Jacque asked. "Is it very dangerous?"

"Yes," Rowan said. "It's a sharp, narrow cliff that drops down over thirty metres to the base of a mountain on the Watertown side. I don't think anyone who fell would survive."

Jacque kept looking up at Raven's Point with a deep frown on his face, as if he were debating making the climb.

Jace had shared his suspicion with Rowan earlier that Victor and Lenny may have been looking for a shortcut for Jacque. So far, it had been the only possible reason for climbing Raven's Point. He decided to try to get some answers out of Jacque. "Why do you want to go up there, anyway?" he asked, as if he were making casual conversation.

Jacque gave him a suspicious look. "What did Lenny and Victor tell you?"

"Not much," Rowan admitted with a shrug.

Jacque was silent and gave Rowan and Jace a look that sent chills down their spines. They both stood still, a little afraid of what Jacque might do next.

"Look," Jacque said finally, pointing his finger at the boys. "I don't know what you know or what you've been told, but listen to me: Mind your own business. If you spread rumours about me, you will pay for it. Understand?"

The boys nodded before Jacque turned and jogged down the mountain, leaving the boys in his dust and a little stunned.

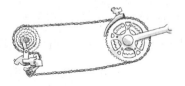

CHAPTER ELEVEN

While the boys were taking Jacque up to Raven's Point, Astrid and Quinn were bored and hoping that Maddie would call and liven up their day.

"I can't even get a signal," Astrid whined as she lifted the phone above her head and walked in a circle. "Maddie could be trying to call right now and she wouldn't get through!"

"I wonder what she's doing today." Quinn sighed dreamily. "I bet whatever it is, it's awesome!"

Astrid lifted the phone above her head and then down towards the ground, willing it to ring. She turned this way and that, nearly walking into the street several times. Finally she shouted, "Oh! I think I've got a signal!"

She took a few more steps, then frowned. "No, it's gone. Wait! There it is!"

Quinn followed Astrid as she walked down an alley, alternating between cheering and pouting as the phone got, and then lost, a signal. The two of them weren't looking at anything except the small phone screen when they turned the corner behind the Sugar Shack. Quinn looked away from the phone and spotted Delilah Downey and Captain Joel Osgood by the shop's back door. She grabbed Astrid's arm, pulled her against the wall and said, "Shhh!"

Astrid's eyes grew wide when she spotted the couple. They were standing very close to each other and wore huge smiles on their faces. Astrid wiggled her eyebrows up and down and whispered to Quinn, "Well, what do we have here?"

Unfortunately, Astrid's whisper was not as quiet as Quinn's had been, and Delilah and Joel both looked up at them. The girls hadn't noticed it before, but they saw the couple let go of each other's hands.

"Hello, girls," Delilah said. Even from the distance, Astrid and Quinn could see that she was blushing.

"Hi, Delilah," Astrid responded. "Hi, Captain Osgood." She waved using the hand that held the mobile phone. She quickly stuck the phone in her pocket as she and Quinn walked towards the pair.

For a moment all four people stood in awkward silence. Then everyone tried to talk at once.

"Nice weather we're having!" Astrid said.

"How's your summer going?" Delilah asked.

"What's new?" Captain Osgood asked.

"Those sweets smell good!" Quinn said.

They all laughed, easing the tension.

"I guess you're wondering what's going on here," Delilah said.

"Well, kind of," Astrid responded.

"But maybe it's none of our business," Quinn added.

Delilah looked at Captain Osgood, who couldn't stop smiling as he looked back at her. He took her hand in his and said proudly, "We've been dating."

"That's wonderful!" Quinn said.

"Congratulations!" said Astrid.

"Thanks," Delilah said, glancing at Captain Osgood. "If it's not too much to ask, we'd like to keep it a secret a little while longer."

"Right. Sure," Astrid said, unable to hide her confusion.

"It's just that if my parents knew, they'd start planning the wedding, and we're not ready for all that yet," Delilah explained. She smiled, squeezed the captain's hand and added, "We've been keeping it to ourselves."

"It's been nice getting to know each other," the captain said, still with his eyes on Delilah. "Sometimes it feels like we're in our own little world."

The couple stood looking dreamily into each other's eyes. After a moment, Astrid and Quinn began to feel uncomfortable in the couple's private world, so Astrid cleared her throat.

"Oh, sorry!" The captain blushed, finally looking away from Delilah. "But I have to say, it definitely feels good to tell someone! I'm not sure how much longer I can keep this a secret."

"I know!" Delilah beamed. "I've been dying to tell people, but I'm just not ready to tell my parents."

"Don't worry about us. Our lips are sealed!" Quinn told them.

"We won't tell anyone," Astrid agreed. She felt the phone vibrate in her pocket. "We'd better go!"

At first Quinn thought Astrid just wanted to leave the two lovebirds alone, but then she heard the phone buzz and understood. She waved to the couple and shouted, "See you later! Glad you're dating!"

Captain Osgood and Delilah exchanged confused looks, but a moment later seemed to have forgotten the girls were even there.

"'*Glad you're dating*'?" Astrid teased Quinn as they turned back around the corner to the alley alongside the Sugar Shack.

"I panicked!" Quinn admitted.

When they were out of sight, Astrid pulled out the phone. It had stopped buzzing. She checked the screen and saw that Maddie had not been calling but had sent a new picture.

"Open it up!" Quinn urged.

Astrid tapped the phone a few times and a picture of a bridge covered with with padlocks filled the screen.

"What is that?" Quinn wondered.

A moment later a text message came through: "This is the Ponts des Arts. Couples in love put padlocks with their initials on the bridge and throw the key into the Seine River. So cool!"

"Awwww!" Astrid and Quinn said at the same time.

Quinn furrowed her brow. "Wait a minute, I thought the city removed those locks?"

"They must not have, otherwise Maddie wouldn't have been able to take this picture," Astrid replied. With a sigh she added, "Maddie is so lucky. Nothing romantic like that ever happens around here!"

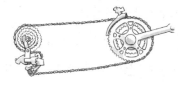

CHAPTER TWELVE

Rowan and Jace had come to a dead end in their investigation of the Big Root Tree Company, and they had been threatened by Jacque Bolive. With the local stage of the race just a day away, they turned to the one person they knew could help them: Mr P.

Mr P was the high-ranking NIA official responsible for Jace and Evie while they were in hiding. While Jace and Evie adored Mr P for all he had done for their family, their friends found him more than a bit odd.

"Hello, children," Mr P said stiffly as he sat at the counter in Mick's Diner.

"Hello, Mr P," Astrid replied in her best robot voice. Rowan shot her a dirty look, but Mr P did not seem to notice, or care, that she was mocking him.

It wasn't unusual for the people of Somerville to see Mr P in town. He had been introduced to most of them as Jace and Evie's cousin who lived not too far from town and visited often.

Mrs Vega spotted him and walked over immediately, her arms open wide to give him a big hug. Mr P was not a hugger in any sense of the word, but had learned to endure Mrs Vega's affection.

"Hello, Mrs Vega," he said as he sat stiffly, awkwardly patting her back while she hugged him.

"How many times do I need to tell you? Please call me Amelia," Mrs Vega replied sincerely. "Let me go and get Evie for you. She's in the kitchen helping Jason. She's becoming quite the cook!"

Mrs Vega hurried off to the kitchen, and Mr P relaxed a little bit, seeming happy to have survived another greeting.

When Evie arrived, the group moved to a back booth where they could have some privacy. As soon as they were seated, Mr P began speaking.

"Jace and Evie, your parents are doing very well. The agency is making progress daily and feels that both you and your parents are very secure. While I don't have a date for their return, they sent a message to you and your friends."

Mr P took out a tablet, and after a few taps the screen lit up. A smiling couple appeared. Although they were standing outside in bright sunshine, they were both dressed for cold weather in bulky sweaters and wool hats. Puffs of cold air came from their mouths. How could this be, when it was summer in Somerville?

The woman had the same green eyes as Jace and a bright smile. Although the man wore a hat, his dark hair poked out from under it and over his eyes. There was no mistaking that this couple was related to Jace and Evie.

"Hello, my loves!" Jace and Evie's mum and dad smiled and waved. "We love you and miss you so much!"

Jace swiped quickly at the tears that began to fall down his cheeks, but Evie didn't bother to hide her emotions and cried openly. Mrs Vega put her arm around Evie and handed her a tissue. Everyone knew Jace and Evie missed their parents terribly and were filled with relief to see them smiling and safe.

"Mr P gives us daily updates, and we love hearing about all that you're doing," their dad said. "After all the travelling we've done as a family, who knew you would like living in a small town so much?"

"We know this hasn't been easy," Jace's mum said. "But it really is necessary. I know we usually send these messages to you privately, but we wanted to say thank you to your new friends for being there for you. It makes us feel so much better knowing you have a strong support system there."

"Yes, thank you Rowan, Astrid and Quinn and your parents. We really appreciate it and can't wait to meet you," Jace's dad added. "We've got to get going now, but we'll send another message soon. Love you, guys!"

In a flash the tablet went blank.

Quinn playfully punched Jace in the arm and smiled. They all sat quietly and, aside from Mr P, there wasn't a dry eye at the table.

"May I have a few doughnuts, please?" Mr P said, breaking the silence.

Evie laughed as she wiped her eyes. "Coming right up!"

After Mr P had made his way through several of the restaurant's famous doughnuts, Jace asked, "Did you get any information about the Big Root Tree Company or Jacque Bolive?"

Mr P swallowed, slowly took a sip of coffee and wiped his mouth. "I have looked into the background of every individual associated with this race and did not find any of them to be a threat."

He paused to take another sip of coffee. "Having said that, I can tell you that the Big Root Tree Company is in terrible shape. They have lost money year after year, and their sponsoring of a stage in a professional cycling race is honestly quite baffling. The only reason I can think of is they are making a last-ditch effort to bring in more business. If it doesn't work, they will certainly be out of business within a year."

"What about Jacque?" Jace asked.

"As I'm sure you know from the news, he has fallen on hard times and is making a halfhearted attempt to get back into the cycling world," Mr P said. "He does not appear to be a man of high morals, but from the research I've done, he doesn't appear to be a danger."

Jace and Rowan exchanged glances. They had not told Mr P about Jacque's threats or their visits to Raven's Point. They feared Mr P would make Jace and Evie leave Somerville if it looked like the bike race was threatening them.

Mr P asked, "Why are you asking about the Big Root Tree Company and Jacque Bolive?"

"Um, well," Jace stammered. "You know I've always been a big cycling fan."

"Yeah," Rowan added. "Jace has been super-excited about the race coming through town, so we've been researching the teams."

Mr P squinted suspiciously at the boys, but didn't ask any more questions. He took a final sip of his coffee and got up from the table. "Goodbye, then," he said and left abruptly.

"That is one strange guy," Astrid said as she watched Mr P walk out of the door. The foursome got up from the booth.

They walked past the only other occupied table, where Mrs Arlene Studebaker was sitting with Ms Patty Meyers, the mayor's secretary. Mrs Studebaker ran the counter at the town's post office and was a huge gossip.

"I know it's not even lunchtime, but I just had to get out of there!" they heard her say. She appeared to be worked up about something, waving her hands wildly as she talked.

"What's the Big Root Tree Company?" Ms Meyers asked. "I've never heard of them."

This got the foursome's attention. Astrid, Quinn, Rowan and Jace froze near the table where the ladies sat.

"I have no idea, but whoever they are, they just had an enormous box arrive for them that has LIVE INSECTS written in huge letters on the side of it." Mrs Studebaker shivered at the mention of it.

Mrs Vega came over and chatted with the ladies. The talk quickly moved from insects to baked goods. The kids made their way out of the restaurant.

"Live insects?" Astrid asked when they were all outside.

"What is that all about?" Quinn wondered.

"I don't know," Rowan said. "But I think we should get over to the post office and check it out."

CHAPTER THIRTEEN

In a town as small as Somerville, you wouldn't expect the post office to be a very busy place, but on this day a queue stretched out of the door. Rowan, Jace, Quinn and Astrid waited not-so-patiently behind tourists looking for postcard stamps and locals needing to send packages.

As they got closer to the counter, they heard Mike Reynolds, the post office manager, apologizing to the people in the queue. "Sorry, folks! I'm not sure where Arlene ran off to, but I'm moving as fast as I can!"

By the time the kids got to the front of the queue, the crowd had died down and the manager looked exhausted.

"Hi, Mr Reynolds," Rowan began cheerfully, realizing he had no idea how they were going to get to the Big Root Tree Company's package.

"Hello, kids," Mr Reynolds replied, barely lifting his eyes from the stack of post he was sorting.

"Have any strange packages arrived lately?" Rowan asked.

Mr Reynolds looked up. "Are you expecting something for someone?"

"Well, you see . . ." Rowan hesitated.

"Feel free to look in the back," Mr Reynolds said hurriedly. "I have no idea where Arlene is, and I've got to get out and deliver this post soon or I'll be out all night!"

Not wanting to jinx their good luck, the kids walked around the counter and into the back room.

They spread out and began scanning the boxes on the shelves.

"Here it is!" Astrid said in a loud whisper, and the others ran over to where she was standing. Alone on a shelf sat a white box addressed to the Big Root Tree Company, care of the Somerville Post Office. As Mrs Studebaker had said, the words LIVE INSECTS were written on each side.

"Do you see any other information?" Rowan asked, scanning the box.

"I'm not touching it!" Astrid told him.

Rowan huffed in annoyance. "Then get out of the way! I'll do it."

Rowan turned the box and found some information on the side, but as they began reading it, Mr Reynolds came into the back room, carrying his postbag.

"Did you kids find what you're looking for?" he asked. "Arlene's still not back from her lunch break, and I need to lock up the post office so I can get going on my route."

Quick as a flash, Astrid pulled out the mobile phone and snapped a picture of the information on the box.

"No, must not have come in yet," she said.

"Thanks for letting us look," Rowan added, and the foursome hurried out of the post office.

When they were out on the pavement, Astrid beamed with pride. "See? I told you a phone would come in handy!"

"Congratulations," Rowan replied sourly. "Let me see the picture."

Rowan enlarged the picture so he could study it better.

"What does it say?" Quinn asked.

"It says the box contains live mountain pine beetles," Rowan said.

"Beetles?" Jace questioned. "Maybe we *did* hear Lenny and Victor right when we thought they were talking about beetles. Let's go back to my house and look them up online. Hopefully we can figure out what this has to do with a bike race."

Back at the Potters' place, Jace pulled up information about mountain pine beetles on his computer.

"It says here that as few as one hundred of these beetles can destroy a whole forest of trees," Jace read.

"Destroy trees?" Quinn asked. "Why would a company that helps trees be interested in beetles that destroy them?"

"Maybe they are buying up all the mountain pine beetles in the world so they can kill them before they harm any trees?" Astrid suggested. Quinn, Rowan and Jace all turned their attention away from the computer screen and looked at her as if she'd gone mad.

"Oh, come on," Astrid protested. "It's not like any of you have a better guess!"

Rowan paced the room. "What I also want to know is, what does this have to do with the bike race or Somerville?"

As the four considered this, Astrid's phone buzzed again. She tapped the speaker button.

"G'day, mate!" said Maddie.

Quinn asked, "You're in Australia?"

"Yes!" Maddie said. "We're having so much fun!"

"Australia?" Jace said. "Weren't you just in Paris? Australia is a long way from France."

"They fly on a jet," Astrid said, as if that explained it. Jace looked doubtful but kept quiet.

"What's new?" Maddie asked. "Any luck solving your mystery?"

Astrid flinched. She knew Rowan had been annoyed when she'd told Maddie about Victor and Lenny. She didn't want him getting mad again. But Rowan didn't mind that Maddie knew and, in fact, wondered if an outside perspective might be helpful. He told Maddie about the beetles.

"Hmmm," Maddie said after he'd finished. "I wonder if they are trying to cheat."

Rowan and Jace exchanged glances. They had both been suspecting that Victor, Lenny and Jacque might be cheating, and hearing someone else have the same thought made their hunch stronger.

If Maddie had that same idea, perhaps they were on to something.

Before they could discuss it any more, a muffled voice could be heard over the phone line and Maddie said, "I'd better get going. It's time to eat."

"Wait. Isn't it, like, the middle of the night in Australia?" Quinn asked.

"Yeah. We've been travelling so much our schedule is all mixed up," Maddie said, chuckling. Before hanging up, she quickly added, "I'll call you tomorrow! Can't wait to hear all about the race!"

"What now?" Astrid asked after she'd put the phone in her pocket. "The riders will come tomorrow, and we have no idea what Lenny and Victor are up to."

"Well, we know it's no good," Rowan snorted.

"Rowan and I had thought maybe Victor and Lenny were trying to help Jacque cheat in some way," Jace said. "Maybe they were looking for a shortcut for Jacque."

Astrid let out a laugh. "Well, if Jacque falls off Raven's Point and into River Forest below, he'll definitely get to Watertown before the rest of the riders. He may not be alive, but he'll be there!"

"Why would Victor and Lenny want to help Jacque cheat? What's in it for them?" Rowan asked.

"Money," Jace responded. "The winner of each stage is awarded a prize, and the team that wins overall gets an even bigger prize. Maybe Jacque has agreed to cut them in if he wins."

"I still don't understand how climbing Raven's Point is going to help," Astrid sighed.

Quinn furrowed her brows. "Maybe there is a shortcut, and we just don't know about it? None of us have ever been to the top of Raven's Point."

Jace, Rowan and Astrid all nodded.

"That's true," Rowan said. "I guess we'll find out tomorrow."

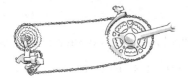

CHAPTER FOURTEEN

Race day was here, and the town was abuzz with anticipation. The people of Somerville set up deckchairs up and down the High Street so they could catch a glimpse of the riders as they raced by. From the look of it, one might think it was St Patrick's Day and the parade was about to start.

Before the Tour Across the Land stirred up interest, there hadn't been many cycling fans in

Somerville. But the *Gazette* had put out a special edition featuring the biggest teams in the race. Now everyone in town had a favourite team or rider to cheer for.

Most residents picked favourites based on their names or colours. Riders came from all over the world, and local fans wanted to show support. They waved little flags and wore T-shirts bearing the names or colours of France, Germany, Italy, Ireland and many more countries. Perhaps the biggest fan was Mr Rossi, who wore a gigantic Italian flag draped over his shoulders. He was keeping an eye out for Lorenzo Ferrari, a very popular rider from Palermo, Italy. That happened to be the very place from which Mr Rossi's great-grandparents had emigrated.

Mick's Diner was busy that morning as people loaded up on cold drinks, sandwiches and baked goods before settling outdoors to watch the racers pass. Astrid and Rowan had been busy boxing up doughnuts and pastries and pouring fresh-squeezed lemonade and hot coffee into take-away cups.

Things were slowing down when Jace and Quinn finally arrived.

"Nice jersey," Rowan said to Jace. He was dressed in his favourite Indulge Cycling racing jersey.

"Thanks!" Jace smiled. He was looking forward to the race but anxious about finding out what Lenny and Victor were up to. He whispered to Rowan, "Have you seen Lenny and Victor?"

Rowan looked around to make sure no one was listening. "Nope, haven't seen them."

Mrs Vega came up behind them, startling Rowan.

"Hey, jumpy!" she teased and put her arm around her son. "Thanks for your hard work this morning. Do me a favour and take some lemonade out to Miss Coco and Mrs Partridge. Then you can go and enjoy the race."

"Thanks, Mum," Rowan said and headed out.

Directly in front of the restaurant, Miss Coco sat in a fancy deckchair that had a giant umbrella attached to it. She wore a floppy straw hat, enormous sunglasses and, despite the heat of the day, a spring jacket. Next to her sat Mrs Ruth Partridge in a less elaborate chair with her loyal dog, Rex, perched like a prince on her lap.

"Oh! Isn't this exciting?" Miss Coco beamed as she took in the scene. "This reminds me of the Gold Rush. I used to sit on the side of the road like this with my sisters and watch the Forty Niners pass by in their covered wagons on their way to finding their fortunes in California. Sometimes they struck gold! What a thrilling time."

As the curator of the town's museum, and an avid history buff, Mrs Partridge knew all about the California Gold Rush of the mid-1800s. She turned to her old friend in bewilderment and said, "What are you talking about? You weren't even alive during the Gold Rush! For that matter, Somerville hadn't even been founded yet!"

"Hmmmm?" Miss Coco pretended not to hear her as she turned her head in the other direction and began loudly humming a tune, quickly putting an end to their conversation.

"Hello, ladies," Rowan said, handing them each a glass of ice-cold lemonade. "My mum wanted me to give you these."

"And these are for Rex," Jace said, handing Mrs Partridge a bowl of ice cubes.

"Oh, thank you," Mrs Partridge said as she took the bowl. "We wouldn't want poor Rex here to get overheated."

Behind her big sunglasses, Miss Coco rolled her eyes over the way her friend spoiled her dog.

Just then Quinn and Astrid rode past on their bicycles. Astrid slowed and said, "We found a spot on the corner where we can watch the race go by. Meet us down there."

Jace and Rowan fetched their bikes from behind the restaurant and met up with the girls. When they were together, they huddled up to discuss their plan.

"We'll stay here and watch the racers go by," Rowan said in a hushed voice. "Then we'll take the shortcut up to Raven's Point to see if anything is going on."

The others nodded as a loud cheer erupted from the crowd.

"Here they come!" they heard someone shout.

All heads turned in the same direction, straining to catch a glimpse of the oncoming riders. In the distance, two cyclists grew larger and larger as they approached.

"I think that's Jan Eldridge!" Jace called.

Jace roared as Jan and another rider approached. The other rider was Lorenzo Ferrari, and as soon as Mr Rossi realized it, he jumped up from his chair. He ran alongside Lorenzo, waving his flag and cheering the rider on. Mr Rossi was not in great shape, however, and after about thirty metres he stopped and put his hands on his knees, panting. Everyone loved Mr Rossi's enthusiasm, and once he caught his breath, he waved and smiled at the crowd, who cheered at him.

There was a brief lull after all that excitement, and the crowd was confused for a moment before someone yelled, "Here come some more!"

A much larger group of riders rode through, along with some team cars that were available to hand out water to the riders and support them in case of a breakdown or crash. Rowan spotted Lenny and Victor across the street. The men were keeping a close eye on Jacque, who had slowed down to wave to the crowd, much to the annoyance of the other riders.

"There they are!" Rowan told the others.

As soon as the racers passed, the foursome saw Lenny and Victor take off. Rowan put on his helmet and turned towards the others. "Let's go!"

CHAPTER FIFTEEN

Inspired by the racers they had just watched speed down the High Street, Astrid, Quinn, Rowan and Jace raced up the shortcut to Perkin's Outlook. As they stopped to catch their breath and drink water, they debated what to do next.

"I guess we should hide our bikes so they don't know we're here, and head up to Raven's Point," Rowan offered.

They hid the bikes behind some large rocks near the car park and covered them with branches. Then they began the climb to Raven's Point.

Near the warning signs, the foursome stood looking up at the remaining climb. The wind blew against their backs, and they could tell a storm was heading their way.

Having been told her whole life to stay away from Raven's Point, Quinn questioned coming so close. "This is really dangerous," she said. "This is a bad idea."

"What are we going to do when they get here?" Jace asked. He turned and spotted dark clouds that were quickly approaching. He knew the rocks they were standing on were slippery when dry. He couldn't imagine how dangerous they would get when wet.

"I don't know," Rowan admitted. He had been so sure Victor and Lenny were doing something wrong, he hadn't thought past catching them in the act. As a light rain began to fall, Rowan felt guilty for dragging the others up to such a dangerous place.

"Let's head back before the storm starts. We can call Captain Osgood for help."

As soon as they turned to head back, they spotted a vehicle in the car park. Even from that great distance, they could see that it was one of the Big Root Tree Company's trucks. When they looked closer, they could see Victor and Lenny making their way up the trail to Raven's Point – straight towards them.

"Quick! Hide!" Astrid said.

All four of them looked frantically for a place to take cover. There was a large boulder just past the warning signs, and they could all crouch behind it. They huddled together and waited.

They heard the men panting and gasping as they came near.

"Where is he?" Victor barked.

"I don't know," Lenny admitted. "He should have beaten us here. Maybe those pesky kids didn't show him the right place!"

Rowan and Jace exchanged worried glances.

"That good-for-nothin' cheat better show up or I'm not paying him!" Victor said furiously.

After a few minutes they heard Lenny's voice again. "Here he comes!" he said.

"Where have you been?" Victor yelled. "If we're not at the finish line to greet the riders, it's going to look suspicious!"

Even though he had cycled several kilometres up the mountain and climbed the trail on foot, Jacque didn't even sound winded.

"Did you want someone to see me riding off the route?" he asked angrily. "I faked a leg cramp and waited for the others to pass. Who knew there would be so many pathetic riders that would make me wait so long."

"Did anyone see you?" Victor asked.

"Of course not!" Jacque snapped. "Hurry up. Give me the beetles. I don't want to finish in last place."

"Like it really matters," Victor said. "I'm paying you more money to do this than you'd make if you somehow managed to win."

"Are you suggesting I couldn't win a race like this?" Jacque said.

"Not without cheating," Victor replied.

Rowan peeked around the boulder in time to see Jacque lunge for Victor.

"Guys!" Lenny said. "We're here to do a job. Now let's get it over with so we can get out of here. That storm looks like it's coming in quick."

Right on cue, lightning crackled above and the skies opened up. Sheets of rain poured down.

"Okay," Victor shouted over the falling rain. "Here's the deal: You need to take this box over the pass and release the beetles among the trees below."

"Fine," Jacque muttered.

From behind the boulder, the kids spied Jacque trying to get his footing so he could begin the steep climb to the top. He slipped several times and kept wiping the rain from his eyes.

The rain continued to fall.

"It's too wet to climb," Jacque complained. "I could barely get up there when the rocks were dry.

There's no way I can do it now. Why don't we release the beetles here?"

"It won't work!" Victor shouted. "We hired you because you're the only one strong enough to climb that pass and release them in the right place!"

"Breaking my neck was not part of the plan!" Jacque shouted. "This whole thing seems pretty stupid to me!"

"Oh yeah, smart guy?" Victor bellowed. "Who do you think is going to replant all those trees once they die? Us! We'll make a mint! Not such a dumb plan now, is it? Now, if you want that money, you will get moving – now!"

Jacque stood, shaking his head. After a moment, he turned to face the pass.

Astrid, Quinn, Rowan and Jace exchanged glances that said, *What do we do now?* As much as they wanted to stop this evil, tree-killing plan, they had no idea how.

Before they could make a move, they heard rocks shift as Jacque came near them to use the boulder to hoist himself up the cliff. As he pushed off the boulder, he caught sight of them out of the corner of his eye and was so startled he slipped and fell.

"What's going on here?" he demanded.

Astrid, Quinn, Rowan and Jace may not have known what was going on, but whatever it was, they were about to become a part of it.

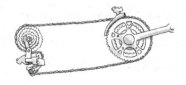

CHAPTER SIXTEEN

Jacque was shocked to see the foursome hiding behind the boulder. He scuttled away quickly.

"What's going on over there?" demanded Victor as he lumbered towards the boulder.

Jacque regained his composure and jumped up. "Those kids who showed me to this place are here! What is going on?"

"What?" Victor snapped at Jacque before turning towards the kids. "Get out from behind there! What are you doing, and how much did you hear?"

Jace, Rowan, Astrid and Quinn stood up and slowly walked out from behind the boulder. They stood in a line in front of Victor, all looking at the ground. They could tell by the tone of his voice that Victor was not happy to see them.

"We, uh, we were just hiking," Rowan said, his voice barely above a whisper.

"A hike?" Jacque asked incredulously. "You were the one who told us this place was dangerous, and now I'm supposed to believe you hike up here? Did the cycling committee send you up here to spy on me?"

"What? No!" Jace replied. "We were just, uh, hanging out."

Victor, Jacque and Lenny crowded around the kids. "Even if you were just hanging out," Victor growled, "we can't let you go back and tell anyone about us being up here."

"We won't tell anyone! Our lips are sealed," Astrid said as she pantomimed locking her lips shut and throwing away the key. "Super-glued shut! We won't tell a soul! Even if they tortured us. We'll take it to our graves."

Rowan didn't want her to give them any ideas by using words like "torture" and "grave", so he kicked her to quieten her down.

"Ouch!" She shot her brother a dirty look. Even in the scariest of times, Astrid and Rowan could have a fight.

"Just let us go and we won't say a word," Jace said as calmly as he could. He was hoping the men couldn't see that he was shaking.

"Maybe we should do that," Lenny said as he looked at Victor and shrugged.

Victor squinted and looked threateningly at each of them. "Maybe."

"No way!" Jacque argued. "If word gets back to the cycling committee about this, I'm ruined! We can't just let them go!"

Victor glared at Jacque. "What do you suggest?"

An evil smile crossed Jacque's face. "Make *them* climb the pass and release the beetles. Then they'll be criminals, too."

Astrid let out a little squeak. She had never been so afraid. She had seen what a hard time Jacque, a trained athlete, had experienced when he tried to climb. There was no way they could safely make it up. And if they did, then what? She'd heard that the cliff at the top was even scarier!

Just then Astrid had a brilliant thought: *I know! I'll use my phone to call for help!*

The phone was in her back pocket, and she decided to slowly take it out and dial 999 behind her back. She may not have been able to say anything, but hopefully the person on the other end would be able to trace the call and send help, like she'd seen in films.

As Victor, Lenny and Jacque debated their plan, Astrid took a deep breath and moved a hand towards her back pocket.

As she tried to remove the phone, Rowan saw what she was doing and shook his head.

Astrid ignored her brother and slowly brought the phone out of her pocket. Once she had it, she searched for the button to wake up the phone. As she moved it around in her hand, the phone got wet from the falling rain and became slippery. Just as she found the button to switch it on, it slipped from her hand and fell to the ground with a thud.

All three men looked at Astrid.

"What's going on?" Victor asked. "What was that?"

Rowan glared at Astrid. She turned away from him and lightly put her foot on the phone to cover it up.

When no one responded, Victor said to Lenny and Jacque, "Okay, fine. Send them up to release the beetles."

Victor and Jacque started towards the foursome, but Lenny stayed behind, holding the box.

"Come on, Lenny!" Victor growled. But Lenny didn't move.

"Are you sure this is a good idea, boss?" he asked.

"Got a better one?" Victor responded.

As the two men argued, Astrid slowly reached down and picked up the phone. No one seemed to notice as she re-pocketed it.

Lenny still didn't move. "I just don't see how making them go up there is going to keep them quiet. They could get really hurt."

Victor looked at the four petrified kids and said, "They're young. They'll be fine. Plus, it will remind them of what we're capable of if they decide to tell anyone – *ever!*"

Rowan, Jace, Astrid and Quinn flinched at Victor's threat. They stood trembling, not sure how to get away.

Lenny didn't have a better idea, so he sighed deeply and carried the box over and handed it to Jace. He knew what they were doing was wrong and couldn't even look Jace in the eye.

"Now get going!" Victor ordered. "We've already wasted enough time. Take the box to the top, open it and send the beetles down the cliff. You do your job, they'll do theirs. Got it?"

No one moved.

"GOT IT?" Victor's face turned red.

Jace turned with the box and saw that Quinn was crying. "I'll do it alone," he said.

Quinn smiled at him gratefully but replied, "We all got ourselves into this, and we'll help each other get out of it."

The climb was harder than they expected, but they supported each other and climbed about a third of the way up.

"Hurry up!" yelled Victor.

Astrid stepped on a rock that gave way, and she slipped and twisted her ankle.

"Ow!" she cried, falling to the ground and clutching her foot.

Rowan climbed over to her but knew there was nothing he could do.

"What are we going to do?" she asked him. "I don't see how we're going to get that box up there.

How will we climb and carry it at the same time? But I don't know what they'll do to us if we don't!"

Rowan frowned. Just then a large bolt of lightning raced across the sky and the rain poured down with even more force.

Astrid shook her head. "We'll never get up now!"

Just then they saw another flash of light cross the sky, but there was no thunder. They looked in the direction it had come from and saw it again. Suddenly they realized the light wasn't lightning, but rather the beam from a torch.

"Stop climbing!" Rowan shouted to Quinn and Jace.

"Keep going!" Victor ordered. "Or else!"

The beam of light was coming from behind the men, and they didn't notice until it was too late.

"Freeze!" Captain Osgood said, drawing his weapon as he approached. "Put your hands where I can see them."

A moment later, three other police officers ran up behind the captain.

Victor, Lenny and Jacque looked around desperately, but there was nowhere for them to go. They put their hands in the air. The officers put them into handcuffs and waved the kids down to safety.

"It worked!" Jace said as he and the others made their way slowly down the hill while helping Astrid.

"What worked?" Quinn asked.

Jace explained, "Mr P gave me these shoes when we moved to Somerville. He told me if I was ever in trouble I should tap the toes together five times and heels together twice and it would send out a call for help. Everyone was distracted when Astrid dropped her phone, so I did it then."

"See?" Astrid said with a weak smile. "I told you I needed a phone!"

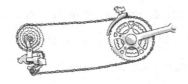

CHAPTER SEVENTEEN

"How many more days of this torture do we have?" Astrid whined.

As proud as their parents had been of Astrid, Rowan, Jace and Quinn for their well-intentioned plan to stop Lenny and Victor, they had also been upset at them for going to Raven's Point alone. When Captain Osgood brought them back to Mick's Diner, Mrs Vega didn't know whether she wanted to strangle or hug them. In the end, she went with very firm hugs. But for the next two weeks, the only place any of them was allowed to be was at their respective homes or at the restaurant, where someone could keep an eye on them.

Even when they were together at the restaurant, they were limited in what they could do because of Astrid's sprained ankle. She had to use crutches when she walked, and when she sat, her leg needed to be propped up. Dr Ramsey said she was very lucky that she got help when she did or the injury would have been much worse.

To add to their annoyance, the foursome was not allowed to talk about what happened at Raven's Point. Their parents had spoken with Captain Osgood and Mr P and decided that it was best to keep the incident quiet so that no extra attention would be drawn to Jace and Evie. Captain Osgood had been able to bring Victor, Lenny and Jacque to Watertown for questioning, and their police department was going to enforce the appropriate punishments.

But the people of Somerville were always looking for a good story, so the gossip began to fly immediately. As is true with most gossip, the vast majority of the stories were completely false.

"I heard that some riders from the race were up to no good and a bunch of brave kids from Watertown caught them. Isn't it amazing that those smart kids were able to outwit some misbehaving adults? Those kids from Watertown are so clever, aren't they?" Mrs Studebaker said to Ms Meyers one afternoon. It was all Astrid, Quinn, Jace and Rowan could do to stop themselves from correcting Mrs Studebaker and letting her know that it was thanks to *their* bravery and cleverness that Watertown's trees had been saved.

They were all thankful that Mrs Studebaker changed the subject as she and Ms Meyers were leaving the restaurant. "Did I tell you that Marge Goodwin told me she saw Delilah Doherty and Captain Osgood sitting together at the cinema last week? She swears they were holding hands!"

Astrid and Quinn smiled at each other but kept their secret. Out of habit, Astrid checked her borrowed phone to see if Maddie had called or sent a message. She frowned at the blank screen. "We haven't heard from Maddie in days," she said.

"I hope everything is okay," Quinn commented.

"Travelling like that can make you super-tired," Jace said. "I bet she's just got jet lag or something."

Another summer storm had rolled into Somerville. Rowan, Astrid, Jace and Quinn were so wrapped up in their boredom, they didn't notice when a family of four came into the restaurant, soaked after getting caught in the sudden shower.

As her parents and her brother dried off, the girl in the group scanned the restaurant. When she saw what she was looking for, she told her mother she would be right back and walked away.

"Astrid?" she asked quietly as she approached the table.

Astrid looked at the girl, who was small with long blonde hair. While she thought she knew all the kids in Somerville, Astrid was sure she had never seen this girl before. "Um, yes?" she replied.

The girl's face lit up and she said, "And you must be Quinn and Rowan and Jace?"

"Well, he's Jace and I'm Rowan," Rowan said to correct her. "Do we know you?"

"It's me! Maddie!" she said. "We're on our way back from our holiday, and my parents couldn't resist stopping at the restaurant."

As Astrid went to stand up, she winced in pain and sat back down. But even a little pain couldn't temper her excitement at finally meeting Maddie. "It's so great to meet you! Where have you been? We haven't heard from you! How was Australia? And Paris and all the other places you were going?"

"How amazing was Japan?" Quinn asked. "Did you get to ride a bullet train?"

"Did you check out the Catacombs like I told you?" Jace asked.

Maddie looked overwhelmed by all the attention. "Oh, yes, it was all amazing! We saw everything!"

"Wait a minute," Rowan said, looking skeptical. "You've only been gone a couple of weeks and you went to Australia, Japan, England and France?" Rowan knew how much travelling would be involved in a trip like that.

"We, uh, actually we didn't get to Japan. I was wrong about that," Maddie stammered.

"But you sent us pictures of Tokyo," Quinn reminded her.

"Did I? Oh, I must be thinking of somewhere else." Maddie's voice trailed off, and for a moment the group sat in confused silence.

Finally Maddie hung her head and said, "I didn't go to any of those places."

"What?" Quinn and Astrid said at the same time.

"But you sent us all those neat pictures!" Quinn said.

"I found them online," Maddie said quietly.

"I guess that explains why you weren't in any photos," Astrid said with a laugh.

"But why did you lie?" Quinn asked.

Maddie sighed. "Because all we really did was go to my grandparents' house like we do every year," she said. "I love my grandparents, but there are no kids in their neighbourhood and sometimes it gets a little boring. You sounded so excited when I told you we were travelling around the world. I decided to have some fun with it." Maddie frowned. "I'm sorry I lied to you."

Astrid waved her hand and said, "Forget about it! It was fun. Plus we know all about being bored."

"I don't see how!" Maddie told her. "From what I hear, you guys have so much going on. Last time we talked you were about to solve a mystery! I've never solved a mystery in my whole life!"

"Actually, you have," Rowan said.

Rowan explained that when Maddie mentioned Victor and Lenny might be cheating, it convinced them to follow their hunch and catch them in the act.

Maddie was still smiling when a young boy with the same blond hair came over and said, "Come on,

Maddie! Mum and Dad want to know what kind of doughnuts you want." Then in a whisper he added, "Did you get my phone?"

He noticed that Astrid was holding his phone, so he extended his hand to take it from her. Astrid looked at the phone. She hung onto it a little longer than she should have, and Rowan noticed.

"Give him his phone, Astrid, or I'll tell Mum you've had it this whole time," Rowan warned her.

Astrid shot her brother a mean look and reluctantly handed the phone over to Gus. "Goodbye, phone," she said softly.

After Maddie and Astrid agreed to stay in touch and the group had said their goodbyes, Rowan refilled their lemonade glasses and brought over a plate of sandwiches. The storm had picked up, and they could hear the rain pounding on the windows.

"What should we do now?" Quinn asked.

Rowan pulled a sheet of paper out of his pocket. He raised his eyebrows and asked hopefully, "Anyone up for a game of War?"

Astrid, Jace and Quinn exchanged glances. "Sure, whatever," Astrid said finally.

"Great!" Rowan exclaimed. "I brought two decks, so we can all play, and then the winner of each game can play each other."

The friendly competitiveness started up right away. "You're not going to cry again when I beat you, are you?" Astrid teased her brother.

"I'll be crying tears of joy watching you lose!" Rowan responded.

Summer in Somerville might not always be as interesting as it had been the past couple of weeks, but sometimes a card game with friends on a rainy day was all the excitement they needed.

About the Author

Raised in the Chicago suburb of Hoffman Estates, in Illinois, USA, Michele Jakubowski has the teachers in her life to thank for her love of reading and writing. While writing has always been a passion for Michele, she believes it is the books she has read throughout the years, and the teachers who assigned them, that have made her the storyteller she is today. Michele lives in Powell, Ohio, with her husband, John, and their children, Jack and Mia.

Glossary

catacomb underground cemetery; the Catacombs of Paris contain the graves of millions of people from the late 1700s and mid 1800s

endorsement act of an athlete wearing, promoting or using a product, often for money

extravagant going beyond what is reasonable or expected

jet lag extreme tiredness and other physical effects felt by a person after travelling between time zones

magnitude great size or extent of something

monotony tedious sameness

moral belief about what is right and wrong

outlook place offering a view

pass route through a mountain range or over a ridge

ration amount of food or supplies allowed by a government

sponsor company or organization that gives a racer equipment or money to race

tournament series of matches between several players or teams, ending in one winner

veteran person who served in the armed forces

Examine the Evidence

1. Astrid feels as though finding the lost mobile phone is fate telling her to keep it. Have you ever experienced something you felt was "fated"? If yes, explain. Use examples from the text to compare Astrid's feelings with yours.

2. Why do you think Maddie feels like she has to lie to Astrid and Quinn about her holiday? Give specific details from the text to support your answer.

3. There are many plot points in the story that could quickly change how events play out. How might the story be different if, for example, Jacque had fallen while climbing, or the live insects had got out of their crate? Discuss, using details from the text.